Three-Minute Tales

KITTENS

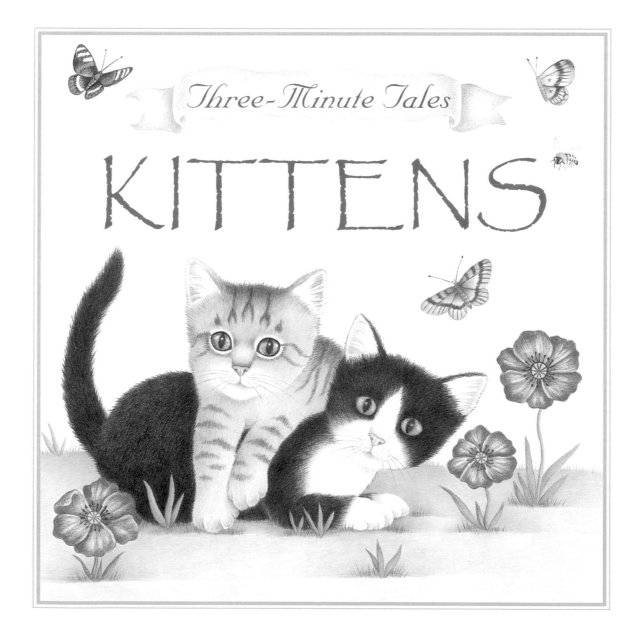

DP
DEMPSEY
PARR

This is a Dempsey Parr book
First Published in 2000

Dempsey Parr is an imprint of Parragon
Parragon
Queen Street House
4 Queen Street
Bath, BA1 1HE, UK

Produced by The Templar Company plc
Pippbrook Mill, London Road, Dorking,
Surrey, RH4 1JE, UK

Designed by Kilnwood Graphics

Printed and bound in Spain
ISBN 1 84084 878 2

Three-Minute Tales

KITTENS

Written by Caroline Repchuk • Illustrated by Stephanie Boey

CONTENTS

Katy and the Butterfly

One Dark Night

Chalk and Cheese

The Disappearing Trick

KATY AND THE BUTTERFLY

As Katy Kitten lay dozing happily in the sun, something tickled her nose. She opened an eye and saw a butterfly hovering above her whiskers. She tapped at it with her soft paw, but it fluttered away. Katy sprang after it and landed with a howl in a bed of thistles, but the butterfly had gone.

"I'll catch that butterfly!" she said, crossly.

Katy chased the butterfly down the garden
towards the stream, where it settled on the
branch of a tree. She climbed up into the tree
after it, higher and higher, but every time she

came near, the butterfly simply flew away.

By now, Katy had climbed so high that she

realised she was quite stuck! Nervously,

she looked down at the stream swirling below her.

Just then, the butterfly fluttered past her nose.
Without thinking, Katy swiped at it with her paw.
But as she did so, she lost her balance and
went tumbling down through the tree, landing
with a great SPLASH! in the water below.
"Help!" cried Katy, waving her paws wildly.
Luckily she caught hold of a branch hanging
over the stream and clambered onto the bank.

Katy arrived home, cold, wet and limping. Her fur was tangled and she was scratched all over. She curled up in front of the fire, feeling exhausted and started to doze. Just then, she felt something tugging at her whiskers.

She opened one eye and saw a little mouse.
"Oh, no, I've done enough chasing for one
day, thank you," said Katy. And with that,
she simply closed her eyes, fell fast asleep,
and dreamt about chasing butterflies!

ONE DARK NIGHT

Paws tiptoed out into the dark farmyard.
Mommy had told him to stay in the barn until
he was old enough to go out at night. But he
was impatient. He had not gone far when
something brushed past his ears. He froze,
as the fur on his neck began to rise. To his relief
it was only a bat — plenty of those in the barn.

A loud hoot echoed through the trees —
"Tu-whit, tu-whoo," and a great, dark shape
swooped down and snatched something up.
"Just an owl," Paws told himself. "Some of
those in the barn too. Nothing to be afraid of!"

Creeping nervously on into the darkness, he
wondered if this was such a good idea after all.
Strange rustlings came from every corner
and he jumped as the old pig gave a loud
grunt close by.

Then, all of a sudden, Paws froze in his tracks.
Beneath the henhouse two eyes glinted in the
darkness, as they came creeping towards him.
This must be the fox Mommy had warned him of!
But to his amazement, he saw it was Mommy!
"Back to the barn!" she said sternly and Paws
happily did as he was told. Maybe he would wait
until he was older to go out at night, after all!

CHALK AND CHEESE

Chalk and Cheese were as different as two kittens can be. Chalk was a fluffy white kitten, who liked dishes of cream and lazing in the sun. Cheese was a rough, tough black kitten, who liked chewing on fish tails and climbing trees. Their mother puzzled over her odd little pair of kittens, but she loved them both the same.

One day, Cheese climbed high up on the barn
and got stuck. "Help!" he cried to his sister.
"I don't like climbing!" she said, opening one eye.
"If only you were more like me!" said Cheese.
"You'd be able to help!"

"If only you were more like me," said Chalk, "you wouldn't have got stuck in the first place!" And with that, she went back to sleep. Just then, the farm dog came by. Chalk sprang up as he gave a loud bark and began to chase her.

"Help!" she cried to Cheese, up on the barn.
"I'm stuck, remember?" he cried. "You shouldn't
lie where dogs can chase you." Then Mommy
appeared. She swiped the dog away with her
claws, then climbed up and rescued Cheese.
"If only you were more like me," she said, "you'd
keep out of danger and look after each other."
And from then on, that's just what they did.

THE DISAPPEARING TRICK

Like all little kittens, Smoky was very playful.
One day, she was chasing her ball, when it
rolled under the fence and into the yard on the
other side. Forgetting Mommy's warnings about
the mean dog who lived there, Smoky
squeezed through the fence, just in time to see
her ball disappear into a hole in the grass...

Smoky looked down into the hole, but it was
very deep and there was no sign of the ball.
Just then, she heard a low growl, and turned
to see an angry dog snarling at her.
In a flash, she scrambled into the hole,

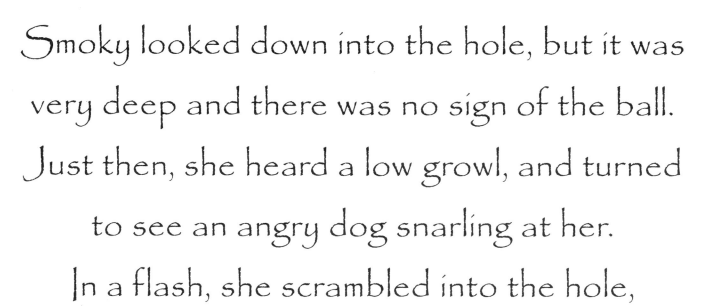

with the dog's sharp teeth snapping at her heels. She squeezed down a long tunnel and into a little room at the bottom. "Hello!" said Rabbit, handing Smoky the ball. "You must be looking for this!"

Smoky was amazed to find she was in Rabbit's burrow. She told him about the angry dog. "Don't worry," said Rabbit, "we'll trick him!" He dug a new tunnel and in no time they were back in Smoky's yard. "Over here!" Rabbit called through the fence to the poor dog still guarding the hole! How the two friends laughed to see the puzzled look on his face.

The End